Copyright © 2010 Flowerpot Press
a Division of Kamalu LLC, Franklin, TN, U.S.A.
and Mitso Media, Inc., Oakville, ON, Canada

American Edition Editor
Sean Kennelly

First Published: 2009

Printed in China.

# CONTENTS

# THE EARTH'S BEGINNING

We live on the Earth. It is a planet that is a part of a group of planets that go around the Sun.

## That's the line-up

The Earth and seven other planets in our solar system go around the Sun that lights up your day. Right next to the Sun is Mercury. Then come Venus, Earth, Mars, Jupiter, Saturn, Uranus and, finally, Neptune.

The Earth is special. It is the only planet we know of that has life on it. Many smaller bodies also go around the Sun. These are called dwarf planets, comets, meteoroids and asteroids.

Each planet has a fixed path around the Sun.

### Fun Facts

From 1930 Pluto was believed to be the ninth planet of our solar system. In 2006 Pluto was removed from the list for being too small. It is now called a dwarf planet or a Kuiper Belt object.

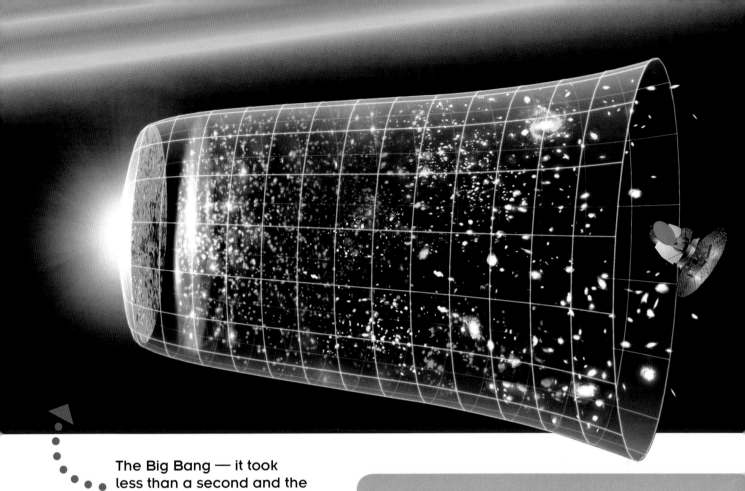

The Big Bang — it took less than a second and the universe was formed.

## How it began

All the planets and stars were once inside a tiny, hot bubble. About 14 billion years ago (that is 14,000,000,000 years!) the bubble burst and particles rushed out of it to form stars. The explosion was so strong that they are still moving away from the bubble. This is called the Big Bang theory. At the time of the Big Bang, the Universe was 1,000 billion degrees Kelvin hot. In one hundredth of a second, it cooled to 100 billion degrees Kelvin.

- Earth and Mercury are the two densest planets in the Solar System. These planets have particles that are more packed together than other planets.

- Though the planet is called Earth, only about thirty per cent of its surface is actually 'earth'. The rest is all water.

- From a distance, the Earth looks the brightest of all planets, because its waters reflect the sunlight.

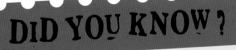

### DID YOU KNOW ?

In one second, the Earth travels about 19 miles (30 km) around the Sun.

# THE EARTH'S INFANCY

The Earth formed millions of years ago. It used to be very different. However, it changed over many different periods.

## Swimmin' around

The earliest period is called the Cambrian Age. It began 570 million years ago and lasted 20 million years. The only life on Earth lived in water. These were soft, invertebrate creatures, or creatures without any backbone. Snails and shelled animals had arrived but the only plant life was seaweeds. Lichen, a plant-like growth, lived on land.

Fossils like this one of the Cambrian Age prove that life existed on Earth millions of years ago.

## Fun Facts

There have been three major eras since the world began:
PALEOZOIC (includes Cambrian, Ordovician, Silurian, Devonian, Carboniferous, Permian periods) *570 – 240 million years ago*
MESOZOIC (includes Triassic, Jurassic and Cretaceous periods) *240 – 65 million years ago*
CENOZOIC (includes Tertiary and Quarternary periods) *65 million years ago – NOW*

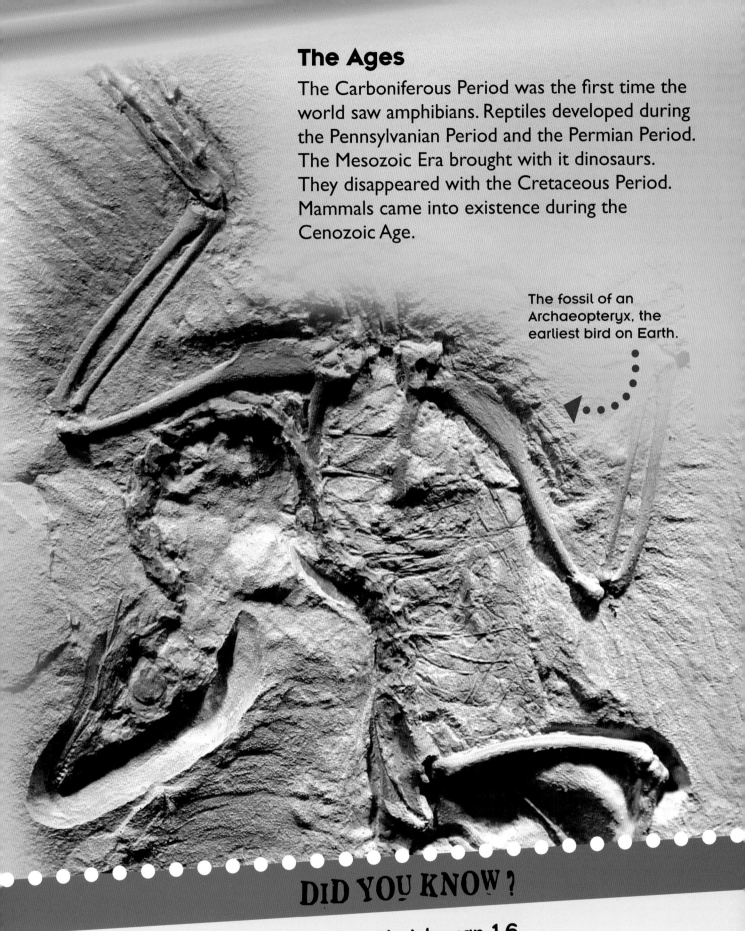

## The Ages

The Carboniferous Period was the first time the world saw amphibians. Reptiles developed during the Pennsylvanian Period and the Permian Period. The Mesozoic Era brought with it dinosaurs. They disappeared with the Cretaceous Period. Mammals came into existence during the Cenozoic Age.

The fossil of an Archaeopteryx, the earliest bird on Earth.

## DID YOU KNOW?

We live in the Quaternary Age that began 1.6 million years ago. All the animals we see around us – even humans – appeared in this age.

# THE EARTH'S STRUCTURE

Have you ever dug a hole in the ground? You'd find soil, pebbles and rocks. But what you see is just the uppermost layer of the Earth.

## Three-tiered Cake

The Earth has three layers. Not all of the Earth is cool enough to live on. Deep down is the core or the center of the Earth. The inner core, which is the hottest part of the Earth, is made up of solid metals like iron and nickel. It is about 1,588 miles (2,556 km) in diameter.

The outer core is also made of iron, but it is liquid. It is about 2,746 miles (4,420 km) thick. Just above the core is the mantle or the middle layer. The inner layer of the mantle is liquid, and so it moves. The outer mantle is cooler and firm.

The mantle that lies below the crust constitutes almost two-thirds of the Earth's mass

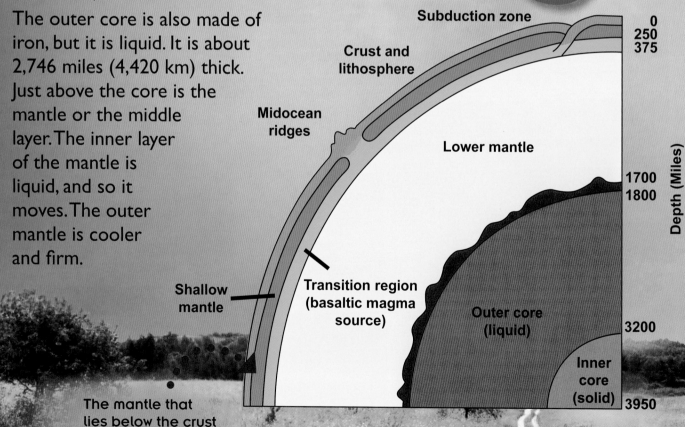

Subduction zone

Crust and lithosphere

Midocean ridges

Lower mantle

Shallow mantle

Transition region (basaltic magma source)

Outer core (liquid)

Inner core (solid)

Depth (Miles)

0
250
375

1700
1800

3200

3950

## That's where we live!

The Earth's surface is called the crust. It is the thinnest layer of the Earth. The crust is made up of rocks, like granite, and water. On the surface are oceans. These cover 70 per cent of the Earth's outermost cover. Some of these oceans can be as deep as 2.5 miles (4 km) in places. As massive as it may seem, the crust makes up less than one per cent of the Earth's total volume.

- Although the crust is a thin layer, it stretches for miles.
- As the Earth's plates move, the land mass of the continents changes. The first ever continent was called Pangea.
- About 245 million years ago in the Triassic Period, the Pangea split when the plates moved away to form the continents of Asia, Africa, Antarctica, Australia, Europe, and North and South America.
- This is why the continents look like pieces of a giant jigsaw puzzle.

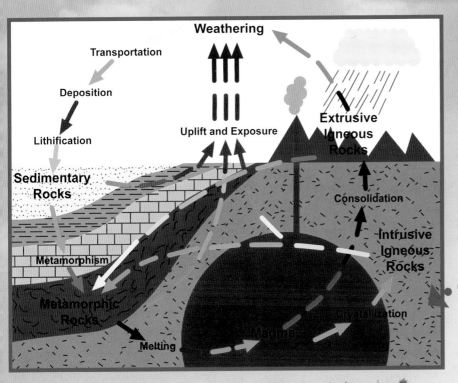

## The Earth's plates

Does the Earth look like one large sheet of soil? It is really made of large sections called continental plates. These plates move slowly over the mantle, covering a few inches in a year.

The Earth's crust is thickest below the continents.

## DID YOU KNOW?

The crust under land (continental crust) is thicker than the oceanic crust that lies under the seas and is barely 6.2 miles (10 km) deep. The continental crust can extend as deep as 56 miles (90 km).

# THE SUN AND LIFE ON EARTH

For billions of years, Earth has had everything needed to support life. Life needs oxygen to breathe, water and the right temperature. It also needs a certain amount of gravity to keep us on the ground.

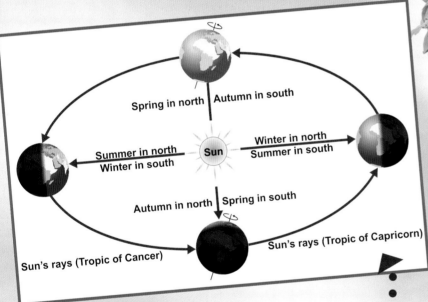

Spring in north | Autumn in south

Summer in north / Winter in south

Sun

Winter in north / Summer in south

Autumn in north | Spring in south

Sun's rays (Tropic of Cancer)

Sun's rays (Tropic of Capricorn)

The Earth going around the Sun.

## Neither too near, nor too far

The Earth is just the right distance from the Sun for us to live on it. If we were any closer, like Mercury or Venus, it would be too hot for life. If we were further away, it would be too cold for life.

## Breathe in, breathe out

Living things are aerobic creatures. This means, they breathe in air. Earth has had oxygen from the time it was created. The atmosphere around the earth is just right for living creatures to breathe in. It is neither too heavy, nor too light. Apart from oxygen, it contains other important elements that life needs, like nitrogen and hydrogen. Some other planets, like Mars, have more of the poisonous gas carbon dioxide than the Earth does.

## The evolution

Early life is believed to have begun in the oceans as simple, single-cell organisms called Protista. Fungi and algae are Protists. As time went by and the Earth cooled, life spread across it. Living creatures also grew in size and became diverse (more different) from each other.

A green Earth makes a healthier environment.

- All living things are made up, in some part, of the element carbon. This is formed when matter burns. Earth had this too, from its explosive birth. Early Earth was so hot that there were many volcanoes that threw up more carbon.

- The force of **gravity** keeps you in place. It also holds the Earth's atmosphere! Smaller planets like Mercury have no atmosphere.

- The temperature on Earth is suitable for life.

- Water supports life. In its natural form, it has no harmful chemicals so we can drink it and forms of life can swim in it.

## DID YOU KNOW?

The part of Earth that has life on it is called the ecosphere.

# WHAT'S ON THE EARTH?

Does the Earth look round to you? It is in fact a little flat at the top and the bottom. The outer crust of the Earth is not smooth. Instead, it has mountains and hills, valleys and plains.

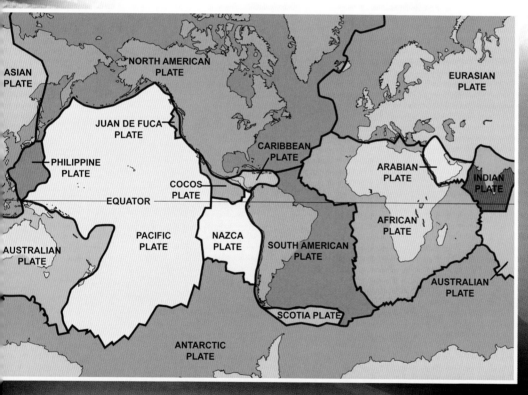

ASIAN PLATE

NORTH AMERICAN PLATE

EURASIAN PLATE

JUAN DE FUCA PLATE

CARIBBEAN PLATE

PHILIPPINE PLATE

ARABIAN PLATE

INDIAN PLATE

COCOS PLATE

EQUATOR

AFRICAN PLATE

AUSTRALIAN PLATE

PACIFIC PLATE

NAZCA PLATE

SOUTH AMERICAN PLATE

AUSTRALIAN PLATE

SCOTIA PLATE

ANTARCTIC PLATE

## Huge patchwork!

The solid part of the Earth or the crust and the outer part of the mantle, is called the Lithosphere. The crust may look like one piece of rock and soil, but it is actually made up of 21 plates. These are constantly moving, hitting each other or slipping away. This is called the Continental Drift

## Always On The Move

The plates have been moving or drifting along for millions of years. Scientists believe the land mass was one piece and the continents have broken apart because of the continental drift. They believe North and South America broke away westwards from what is now the west coast of Europe and Africa.

## Fun Facts

The continental crust under the mountains is the deepest on Earth. It runs to a depth of about 22 miles (35 km) under the Himalayan mountain range, making the thickest area of crust on Earth.

14

The Himalayan mountain range — including some of the highest peaks on Earth.

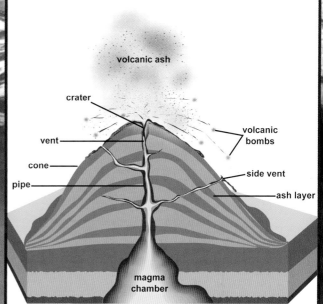

volcanic ash

crater

vent

cone

pipe

volcanic bombs

side vent

ash layer

magma chamber

## Different mountains

When there is a weak spot in the crust or the surface of the Earth (on land or under the sea), the hot, liquid magma below can gush out. These explosive mountains are called volcanoes. The liquid that pours out is called lava.

The Earth's moving plates hit each other with such huge force millions of years ago that they forced rock upwards to form mountains. These formations, like the Himalayas, are called Fold Mountains. When the tectonic plates move suddenly, we feel an earthquake.

- The Earth's crust covers less than one percent of the planet's total volume.
- Lava can reach a temperature of nearly 2192° Farenheit!
- The Earth's plates move up to 4 in (10 cm) per year.

## DID YOU KNOW?

Plate Tectonics is the study of the plates that make up the Earth's crust.

# THE EARTH'S ATMOSPHERE

The Earth is surrounded by different gases that form the atmosphere. The atmosphere is a huge band of colorless gases, dust particles and water vapor that is about 300 miles (483 km) high.

## Do we need it?

The atmosphere acts like a blanket, keeping out harmful ultraviolet rays from the Sun. The atmosphere allows the warmth of the Sun to touch the Earth. But it also keeps some of this warmth trapped so that the Earth stays warm enough to support life. The gases in the atmosphere make up the air that we breathe.

## How did they get there?

The atmosphere was formed when gases like carbon dioxide, nitrogen, sulphur dioxide and water vapor were let out from inside the Earth. There is no exact point where the atmosphere ends. It just gets thinner and lighter and blends into outer space.

### Fun Facts

If you went soaring through the atmosphere in a hot air balloon, you would find it harder to breathe the higher you went as the atmosphere got thinner.

## Layered like an onion

Exosphere: outermost layer of the Earth's atmosphere. Stretches from about 400 miles (644 km) to about 800 miles (1,287 km) high.

Ionosphere: stretches from about 43-50 miles (69-80 km) to about 400 miles (644 km) away from the Earth.

Mesosphere: extends between 31 miles (50 km) to about 50 miles (80 km). The temperature falls quickly the higher you go.

Stratosphere: the belt between 11 miles (18 km) and 31 miles (50 km) above the Earth. This is where the ozone layer is. The ozone layer absorbs harmful rays from the Sun. You'd find high clouds in the lower stratosphere.

Troposphere: the air band closest to Earth, stretching from the surface to about 11 miles (18 km) high. This is where you'd find clouds and weather. Warmest near the Earth, it cools as you travel up. Its upper boundary is called the tropopause.

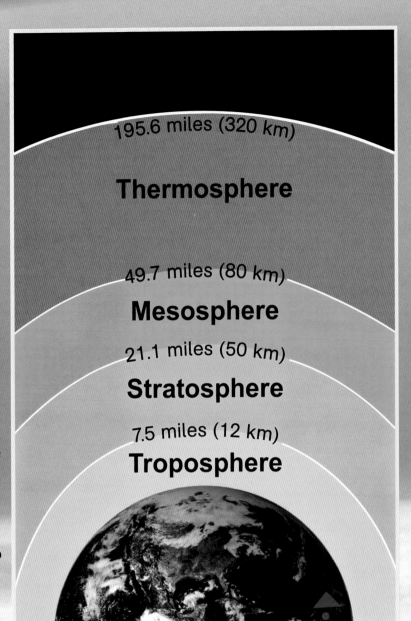

195.6 miles (320 km)

**Thermosphere**

49.7 miles (80 km)

**Mesosphere**

21.1 miles (50 km)

**Stratosphere**

7.5 miles (12 km)

**Troposphere**

The troposphere is where you find life on Earth.

## DID YOU KNOW?

Most of the atmosphere is nitrogen (78 per cent). About 21 per cent is oxygen. Just 0.9 per cent is argon, and carbon dioxide makes up 0.03 per cent. The rest is tiny amounts of other gases.

# THE EARTH'S SURFACE

The surface of the Earth is not even. It has mountains, hills, valleys, plateaus and many more features.

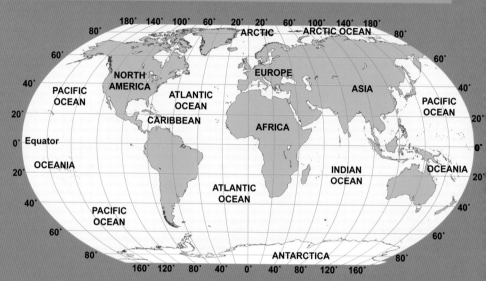

## Continent size

The largest chunks of land are known as continents. The seven continents are Africa, Antarctica, Asia, Australia, Europe, North and South America. The biggest of these is Asia. It covers 17 million sq/miles (44 million sq/km). Asia is home to 3.5 billion people, more than any other continent. The second largest continent is Africa. Then come North and South America.

## It's cold out here

Antarctica is so cold that it is called the frozen continent. It is a bigger continent than both Europe and Australasia. Technically, Antarctica is considered a desert because it gets so little rain!

it is near impossible to live in freezing Antarctica.

## The mountains

Mountains are high structures of rock and soil. The tallest mountain on Earth is Mt. Everest. A hill is a small mountain. The land between two mountains or hills is called a valley. A hill with a large, flat top is called a plateau. Some mountains are also volcanoes – most of which never erupt.

**Fun Facts**

An island is land surrounded by water. An archipelago is a group of islands.

- A plain is flat land.

- A wetland is land that is wet all or most of the time.

- A delta is the land at the mouth of a river. It is made up of sand, silt and rocks that flow down the river.

### DID YOU KNOW ?

The study of how land is formed is called geomorphology.

# IMPORTANCE OF WATER

How did water first appear on Earth? No one is sure. However, one thing is certain: water is essential to the survival of all living beings.

### Where did water first come from?

Some scientists believe water (a chemical combination of hydrogen and oxygen denoted by the formula $H_2O$) formed when the Earth was cooling down and trapped gases were released. Others believe oceans formed when asteroids containing water hit Earth. Still others believe chemical compounds broke down and formed water. Water contains dissolved minerals and gases.

Glaciers and icebergs are frozen water.

# The significance of water

Any form of life on Earth relies on water and we need water for almost all our bodily functions: the blood that flows through the body is part water; food cannot be swallowed or digested without water; plants need water to draw up dissolved minerals from the soil; without water, they cannot make their food through photosynthesis.

sunlight

photosynthesis

sugars

oxygen

carbon dioxide

water

- Water goes around in the water cycle: water vapour gets together to form clouds that drop as rain, snow, hail or sleet. This water fills oceans, caps glaciers or runs underground.
- Plants transpire (breathe out water vapour). Sunlight evaporates water, turning it into gaseous water vapour.
- The droplets of water vapour form clouds once again!

## That's all water!

Water can be in three states: solid ice, liquid or invisible gas or water vapour that forms clouds. Water covers over 70 per cent of the Earth, filling different water bodies. Less than 3 per cent is frozen in glaciers and in ice in the Polar regions.

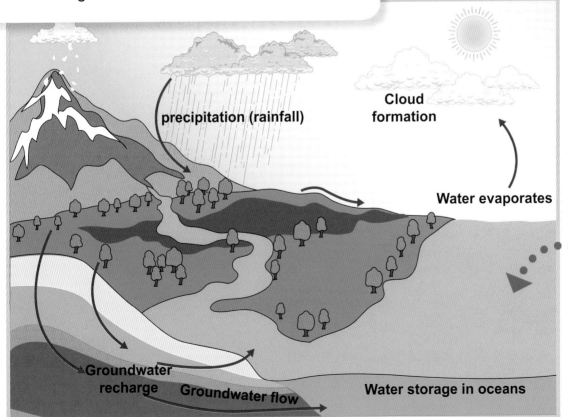

precipitation (rainfall)

Cloud formation

Water evaporates

Groundwater recharge   Groundwater flow

Water storage in oceans

The water cycle — it would be impossible to live without this phenomenon.

# WATER WATER EVERYWHERE

Water, in its liquid form, is found in different waterbodies. There are many types of water bodies in this world, including oceans, seas, lakes and rivers.

## They're the largest!

Over 70 per cent of the Earth's surface is covered by seas and oceans. Although we have given different names to the oceans, they are also recognized as one body of water that scientists call the World Ocean. This World Ocean is one flow of water that is divided into smaller bodies including the Atlantic Ocean, Arctic Ocean, Indian Ocean, Pacific Ocean and Southern Ocean, around Antarctica.

### Fun Facts

The Pacific Ocean is the largest waterbody on Earth. It covers about 105 million sq/miles (169 million sq/km), or over 30 per cent of the Earth's surface!

The Pacific Ocean is the largest body of water in the world.

## Seas, bays and saltwater lakes

A sea is a smaller ocean. Most seas, like the Bering Sea, flow into an ocean. Some, like the Caspian Sea, are saltwater lakes. Indeed, the Caspian Sea is the largest lake in the world.

A bay is water that is partly open to the sea and partly surrounded by land. The Bay of Bengal off the Indian Ocean is the largest bay in the world. Hudson Bay in Canada has the longest shoreline, protected by 7,623 miles (12,268 km) of land.

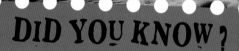

Lake Superior in North America is the largest freshwater lake in the world.

### DID YOU KNOW?

Most of the water on Earth is too salty for us to drink.

## Glaciers

A glacier is a large mass of frozen ice that has formed from layers of snow under pressure. Pressure and gravity force the ice along like a slow-moving river, carving enormous channels through mountains and rocks. About 75 per cent of all freshwater is frozen in glaciers, meaning it would be very dangerous if they were to melt.

At 4,184 miles (6,695 km) long, The Nile is the world's longest river!

# LIVING CONDITIONS

All the natural conditions that affect us make weather: the amount of sunshine; wind direction and its force; precipitation like rain, snow, hail or sleet; the clouds; and even visibility, or how far you can see, all make up the weather.

## What's climate?

The weather over a long period of time is called climate. The climate of an area is determined by its altitude, its distance from the Equator and even by mountain ranges and oceans nearby. When weatherpeople speak of the climate of a place, they take into account up to 30 years of weather data.

## Different seasons

The four major seasons are spring, summer, autumn and winter.

Because the Earth's axis is tilted towards the Sun, the northern and southern halves (or hemispheres) enjoy opposite seasons, depending on which hemisphere is closer to the Sun during orbit.

The four seasons — each different from the other.

## Now it's sunny, now it's not

A noticeable change in weather over some months is called a season. Seasons change as the Earth revolves around the Sun and the tilt of the Earth's axis moves a hemisphere closer to/ further away from the Sun. This alters the amount of light a place gets and creates the weather typical of the seasons.

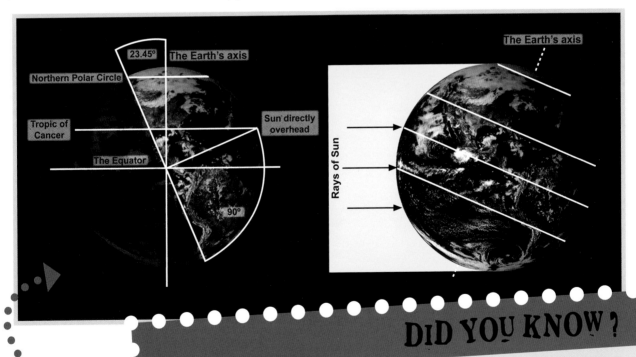

The summer solstice (left) and the winter solstice (right).

# THE EARTH'S HABITATS

Different animals and insects live in different places. Their homes are known as habitats. A place can become a habitat only when it has enough food, water and safety for living things to survive.

### That's where I live!

Most creatures choose one habitat. The snow leopard, for example, is comfortable in the icy heights of mountains. It can survive in the cold because of an unusually thick coat. Its ears and body are smaller in size than a regular leopard, which helps reduce heat loss.

A snow leopard is perfectly suited to the cold environment.

## Different homes

The biosphere is a term that relates to the areas on Earth where there is life. Oceans, lakes, rivers and seas are the hydrosphere. The region under the Earth's surface is called the lithosphere. Each habitat is different. Deserts have sand, rocks and very little water. Mountains have snow, rocks, slopes and barren terrain.

# Diverse animal habitats

The Polar regions, at the northern and southernmost tips of the Earth, are covered in snow. They are home to Polar bears, penguins and seals. Whales, sharks, fish and water plants inhabit the oceans. The desert is home to plants like the cactus and animals like the camel. Frogs, beavers, otters and birds like the egret inhabit the wet marshes. In the rainforests you can find many different species of birds, animals, insects and reptiles.

The magnificent sea turtle.

## Fun Facts

An ideal habitat has enough space, food and water. If too many animals are crowded for space, some have to leave or will die because there's too much competition for food.

## DID YOU KNOW ?

In 1929 a Russian scientist named Vladimir Vernadsky thought of the word biosphere to describe different zones on Earth.

# OPEN TO CHANGE

Animals and plants learn to change so that they can live comfortably.

### I need to grow a tail...

This change over many generations is known as adaptation. Adaptation does not happen overnight. The kangaroo's back legs, for example, have adapted to give it a powerful spring. This gave the kangaroo a powerful jump. Its sturdy tail helps in balancing as well as jumping.

## Fun Facts

Some animals and insects adapt to look like others. This is called mimicry adaptation. The hawk moth looks like a dead leaf so that it can trick its enemies.

### ...or perhaps a longer nose

Animals, birds, insects and plants adapt in different ways. The shape of a bird's beak and its claws help it to eat a particular kind of food. That is why animals have different numbers of fingers and toes or why tails are shapes differently. Insectivorous plants like the pitcher plant and the bladder trap often grow in places where there is little nutrition. So, they have developed ways to trap and digest insects.

## Masters at adapting

The polar bear can live in the very cold polar region because of its thick fur. Its white fur helps the animal camouflage against the white snow. The cactus plant can survive with little water because it has a thick stem that stores water. Because it has few or no leaves, it loses less water by evaporation than other plants.

They may not be pretty, but vultures are nature's cleaning agents!

Polar bears are found in the Poles, where it is near impossible for human beings to survive.

- Coyotes can survive in many different environments as they have the ability to change their breeding habits and diet.

- Goldfish can hear sounds at high frequencies that probably helps them to locate their food.

- Vultures help in cleaning up nature. They scavange the carcasses left by other animals that would otherwise rot.

## DID YOU KNOW?

The polar bear is the largest carnivore found on land. An adult male can weigh up to 1,500 lb (680 kg)!

# INVERTEBRATES ON EARTH

Animals that do not have a backbone or spine are called invertebrates. Most animals are invertebrates. Only about 2 percent of animals have a vertebra or spine.

Snails rely on touch and smell when they are hunting for food.

## Soft but tough

Mollusks make up one of the largest groups of invertebrates. There are over 93,000 species of them. Some, such as snails, live on land and in water. Others, like the octopus, live in water alone.

## Different invertebrates

Flatworms are a group of invertebrates that have soft bodies. Some of them, like tapeworms, live in the digestive system of animals, including humans. Arthropods are a group of invertebrates that have jointed legs. These include insects, arachnids or spiders, and crustaceans or shelled creatures like crabs.

- An earthworm can live on even if it loses a small part of its body.
- Most sponges are sessile, meaning they are fixed in one place.
- Mollusks often use the same organ for excretion and reproduction.

Because they are small, spiders have many natural predators.

## Invertebrates of the sea

Jellyfish and corals belong to the same family of Cnidaria (pronounced nidaria) that have a jelly-like body. Sea urchins and sea cucumbers belong to the Echinodermata family. Like many other echinoderms, starfish move and feed with hundreds of tube feet on the underside of the body. They even have two stomachs.

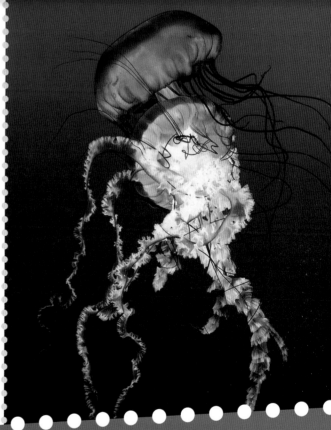

## DID YOU KNOW?

Octopuses are considered the most intelligent invertebrates and can solve complex tasks during scientific experiments.

# EARTH'S ANIMALS

Animals are creatures that have many cells and muscles in their body. Animals cannot make their own food, so they feed on plants or other animals. Most animals can move on their own. Human beings are animals.

Frogs are highly adapted animals.

The tiger is the biggest cat in the world.

## On land and in water

Some animals, like humans, dogs and tigers, live on land. Some, like fish and whales, live only in water. There are some animals, like frogs, salamanders and toads that live both on land and in water. These animals are called amphibians. They are cold-blooded creatures. Since they are cold-blooded creatures, amphibians have to hibernate, or go into a long winter sleep, when the temperature drops.

# Blood runs cold...

Reptiles like snakes, lizards, alligators and turtles are cold-blooded. Reptiles have scaly skin and most of them lay eggs. The king cobra makes a nest to lay its eggs in. Some snakes like the boa constrictor and the green anaconda give birth to live young.

**DID YOU KNOW?**

The word 'animal' comes from the Latin word 'anima', which means breathing.

- Nocturnal animals like the bushbaby can see better in the dark and have a keen sense of smell and sharp ears.
- Animals like the red panda and the rabbit are most active during dawn and at dusk. These are called crepuscular animals.
- The bat may look like a bird but it is a mammal.

## ... or warm

Almost all mammals – warm-blooded creatures – give birth to their babies. Mother mammals feed their babies milk. Most mammals live on land. Some, like whales and dolphins, live in water.

The intelligent dolphins live in water but they do not lay eggs.

# BIRDS

A bird is a warm-blooded, two-legged creature that has a skeleton, beak and feathers. The front two legs have evolved into wings.

## Flying high

Most birds can fly. Although they do walk or hop short distances, flying birds are helped by hollow bones that are light but strong. They have a strong breathing system that also helps them fly.

## Strutting smart

Some birds cannot fly. Many of these birds are found on islands where they have fewer enemies. Some, like the ratites (including the ostrich, emu and cassowary), defend themselves with their sharp claws. Scientists believe that birds may have learnt to fly to escape to safety.

The eagle hunts small birds and animals.

For how long will they be around?

### Fun Facts

There are more flightless birds on the island of New Zealand than anywhere else. These include the kiwi, takahe and penguin.

## Swimming away

Birds like penguins and ducks can dive and swim underwater. Their shorter wings help them paddle. Underwater swimmers like grebes, loons and penguins have heavier bones than birds that fly. This helps them stay underwater. Other swimmers and divers, like pelicans and terns, are also good flyers.

Penguins are birds that can actually swim very well.

This little bird may have evolved from a dinosaur!

- Common loons are among the deepest divings birds, descending up to 500 ft (153 m)!
- The ostrich is the largest bird. It stands about 8.85 ft. high.
- The bee hummingbird lays the smallest egg among birds. Each egg is about the size of a pea! The ostrich lays the largest bird egg. It weighs over 3 lbs (1.3 kg).
- Hummingbirds are some of the best hoverers. They can stay in one place for some time, beating their wings about 52 times a second.

### DID YOU KNOW?

ome birds, like the flightless dodo, have become extinct. This bird was last seen on the island of Mauritius in the late 17th century.

# THE INSECT WORLD

Insects are a class of creatures called arthropods. There are over a million insects that we know of. This makes them the most varied and numerous of all living creatures.

## What-a-pod?

Arthropods have jointed legs and insects have three pairs of those. They do not have a backbone. Instead, they have a hard outer body, or exoskeleton. You'd recognise an insect from its body, which is    divided into three parts: the head, thorax and abdomen. Indeed, the word 'insect' means 'sections' in Latin.

### Fun Facts

Among the arthropods, insects are the biggest group. They are also the only arthropods with wings.

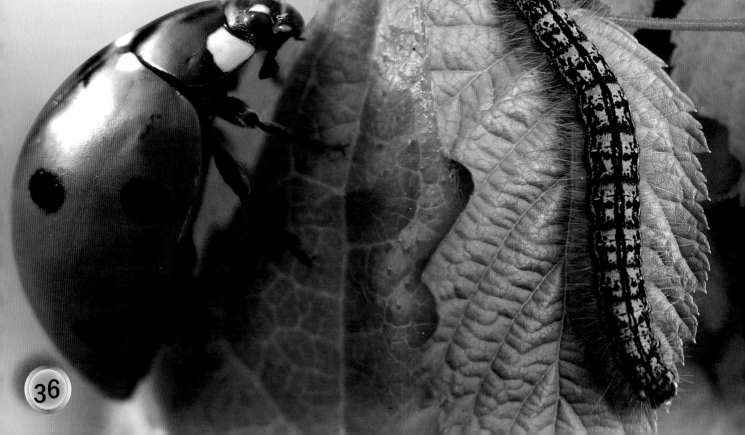

# Different insects

The praying mantis eats other insects. This makes it a friend of the gardener, since it eats up aphids and moths that eat plants. It gets its name from the way it catches its food – remaining motionless with its forelegs pressed together. Like many other insects, it can camouflage itself among plants as it waits for prey. This strange insect can move its head almost all the way around!

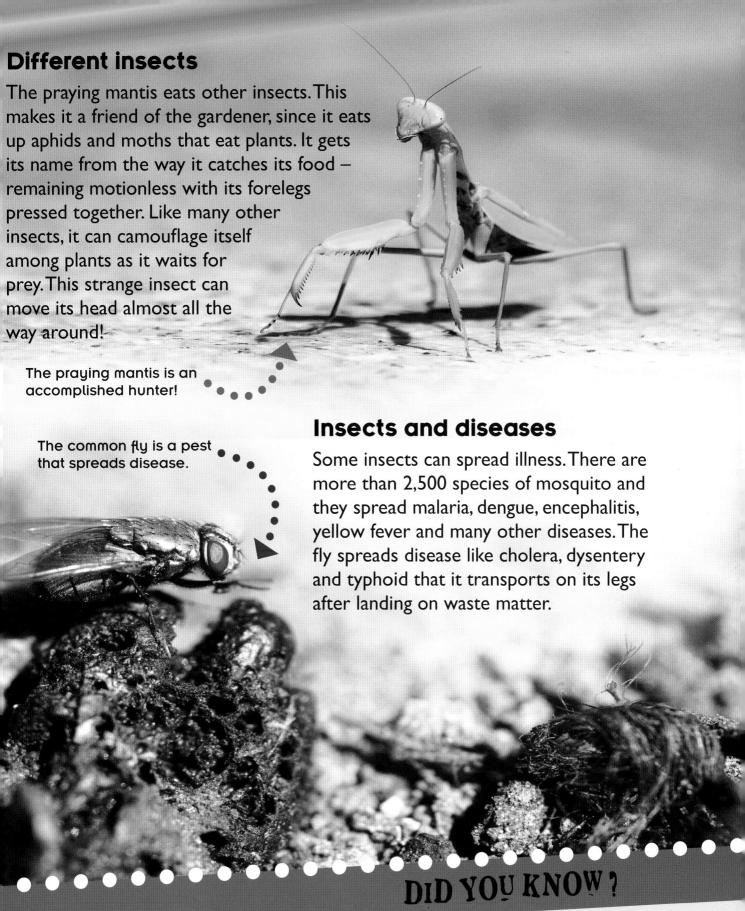

The praying mantis is an accomplished hunter!

The common fly is a pest that spreads disease.

## Insects and diseases

Some insects can spread illness. There are more than 2,500 species of mosquito and they spread malaria, dengue, encephalitis, yellow fever and many other diseases. The fly spreads disease like cholera, dysentery and typhoid that it transports on its legs after landing on waste matter.

## DID YOU KNOW?

You find more insects the warmer the climate. This means the number of insects decreases as you move from the Equator towards the Poles.

# LIFE IN THE WATERS

The first life on Earth began in the sea. Ocean life is diverse. It can be home to microscopic zooplankton or enormous whales.

## Fun Facts

We're still learning about new sea creatures. In 2006, the unusual Promachoteuthis sloani squid was found in the Mid-Atlantic Ridge, which is an underwater mountain range between Europe and America.

## Spineless creature!

Some creatures of the sea don't have a spine. These invertebrates include jellyfish, anemones, mollusks such as squids and octopuses, and spiny creatures or echinodermata like the sea urchin.

# Making bones about it

Fish are among the most common sea creatures, although they also enjoy living in fresh waters. Some, like the hilsa, live in the sea and swim up the river to lay eggs. One of the tiniest fish is the stout infantfish, which is less than half an inch long. At the other end of the scale are sharks. The whale shark is the largest fish and can grow to almost 40 ft (12 m) long. Mammals such as whales also live in the seas. The blue whale is the largest living animal.

## DID YOU KNOW?

Not all fish are safe to eat. The pufferfish has a poison that can paralyze a human.

- Copepods are tiny shrimp-like creatures that are the favorite food of many creatures of the sea.

- The clownfish is one of the few creatures that can live among poisonous anemones.

- The coelacanth has been around for millions of years.

- The cookiecutter shark takes a round bite of its prey's flesh – hence the name.

- Seals and walruses live on land and in the sea.

# PLANT LIFE ON EARTH

Plants are living creatures. They can be as large as trees and as tiny as algae. There are over 287,655 species of plants.

## That's old!

The plant world also includes shrubs and bushes, ferns, mosses, fungi and even some algae. Land plants appeared on Earth around 700 million years ago. As more plants began to grow, they used up more carbon dioxide to make their food by photosynthesis. They also gave out more oxygen, which was necessary for animals to survive.

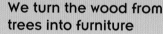
We turn the wood from trees into furniture

## Thank you plants!

Everything we eat comes from, or relies upon, plants. Sometimes it's indirect, when the animals we eat in turn feed on plants. We eat the seeds of plants like rice and wheat. The roots of potatoes, carrots and radishes make nutritious vegetables. Spices like pepper that flavor our food come from plants.

## What's that?

Almost all plants begin from a seed, although some, like ferns, are born from spores. The roots hold the plant firmly to the ground. They also draw up water and dissolved minerals that the plant uses to make food. The stems hold the leaves, flowers and fruit — the seed of the plant. When the seed falls to the ground, it begins to grow into a new plant.

He's actually chewing a plant.

### Fun Facts

Chewing gum is made of chicle, a natural gum from the Manilkara chicle tree that grows in America.

## DID YOU KNOW ?

The study of the uses of plants is known as ethnobotany.

# NATURAL RESOURCES

There are many things in nature that human beings have learned to use. We cannot create natural resources, so we have to use them with great care.

## Protect the rainforests

Forests are among the most important natural resources on Earth, but they are in real danger from humans. The densest forests include the rainforests. These once covered 14 per cent of our land. They have been cut to less than half that and now cover just 6 per cent of the Earth's land surface. If we don't stop cutting them down, they could be gone in less than 50 years.

## Deep underground

Many natural resources are found under the surface of the land or even water. They are dug up by machines and by people. Resources like coal must be mined from deep under the ground. Petroleum – natural oil from the Earth – has to be extracted by drills. Fishing gives us food and oil. Modern fishing trawlers go far into the oceans and trawl the bottom of the seas.

Coal, one of nature's most valuable natural resources, is created from dead animal fossils!

## Earth's resources

Some resources are renewable. Others, like trees and water are sustainable if they are used within limits. There are other resources that are limited in supply because they are being used faster than they are made. These resources, like oil and natural gas, are called non-renewable. Flow renewable resources, such as sunshine, tides and wind can renew themselves. Natural resources like coal and oil, which are fossil fuels made from dead plants and animals, take millions of years to be created.

### Fun Facts

Everything in nature is important. A dead tree provides a habitat to many forms of life from moss and fungus to squirrels, snakes, insects and birds.

## DID YOU KNOW?

Apart from timber, forests give us medicines. Hundreds of medicines are made from plants.

# GLOSSARY

**Asteroids**: floating rocks in space that move around the Sun

**Axis**: imaginary line around which the Earth rotates

**Camouflage**: disguise

**Dense**: something thick where very little light can pass through

**Equator**: imaginary line around the center of the Earth

**Evolution**: process by which something changes over time

**Excretion**: process of discharging unnecessary waste matter from the body

**Earthquake**: shaking and vibration of the Earth's surface

**Gravity**: force of attraction between two bodies

**Hemisphere**: Half of the Earth – divided into Southern and Northern Hemispheres

**Photosynthesis**: process by which plants use sunlight to make their food

**Reproduction**: process of producing young, by birth or other method

**Shoreline**: boundary between water and land

# INDEX